MARVIN
and the
Mean Words

Suzy Kline

MARVIN
and the
Mean Words

illustrations by Blanche Sims

PAPERSTAR

The Putnam & Grosset Group

Acknowledgments

Special appreciation . . .

*As always, for my editor, **Anne O'Connell,** whose questions, criticism, and encouragement helped me develop my story.*

*For my husband, **Rufus,** and my mother, **Martha S. Weaver,** who read many drafts of the story and made suggestions.*

*For my daughter **Emily** and her valuable insight about the relationship between Nonna and Marvin.*

*For my second-grade classes, who visit **The Norman Rockwell Museum** and make it so much fun!*

*For **Thomas Rockwell,** for granting permission to reproduce the following black-and-white prints: **The Runaway** (September 20, 1958) and **Surprise** (March 17, 1956).*

Surprise and The Runaway by Norman Rockwell printed
by permission of the Norman Rockwell Family Trust.

Text copyright © 1997 by Suzy Kline
Illustrations copyright © 1997 by Blanche Sims
All rights reserved. This book, or parts thereof, may not be reproduced
in any form without permission in writing from the publisher.
A PaperStar Book, published in 1998 by The Putnam & Grosset Group,
200 Madison Avenue, New York, NY 10016.
PaperStar is a registered trademark of The Putnam Berkley Group, Inc.
The PaperStar logo is a trademark of The Putnam Berkley Group, Inc.
Originally published in 1997 by G. P. Putnam's Sons.
Published simultaneously in Canada. Printed in the United States of America.
Book design by Donna Mark. Text set in Sabon.
Library of Congress Cataloging-in-Publication Data
Kline, Suzy. Marvin and the mean words / Suzy Kline; illustrations by
Blanche Sims.   p.   cm.   Summary: Marvin overhears remarks made
by his second-grade teacher and is sure she hates him.
[1. Schools—Fiction.   2. Teachers—Fiction.   3. Self-esteem—Fiction.]
I. Sims, Blanche, ill.   II. Title. PZ7.K6797Mak   1997   [Fic]—dc20
96-1450   CIP   AC   ISBN 0-698-11657-7
3   5   7   9   10   8   6   4   2

With love to my daughter Jennifer
and my son-in-law, Matthew DeAngelis,
who exchanged the
most beautiful words
at their outdoor wedding
August 5, 1995

Contents

MARVIN
and the
Mean Words

1

Ants and the Mean Words

Marvin tapped the green ant farm. "I hate her," he said.

"Which one?" Audrey asked.

"Not an ant, HER!"

Audrey turned around.

Marvin was pointing at the teacher.

"Mrs. Bird?" Audrey replied. "You shouldn't say that. She's nice."

"No she's not. She says mean things."

"Marvin!" Audrey scolded. "Our

teacher hasn't said one mean thing in second grade."

Marvin rolled his eyes. "Yes she did."

"When?"

"Yesterday after school. She didn't know I was around the corner getting my jacket."

"Who was she talking about?" Audrey asked.

"Me!" Marvin snapped.

"What did she say?"

"I'm not telling. I'll *never repeat* those words. Ever. They're too mean!"

Audrey made a face. She wanted to know what the teacher had said about Marvin.

Pablo passed out the observation sheets. "We have the greatest committee!"

Fred groaned. "Our ant farm isn't the greatest. There were fifty ants in September. Now it's November, and it's an Ant Cemetery. Just look at all those ant bodies buried in the sand!"

Marvin took his little yellow notebook out of his hip pocket and wrote down a number.

Audrey leaned over his shoulder. "Why do you keep track of things like dead ants?" she asked.

Marvin shrugged.

Fred drew a picture of the dead ants in the lower tunnel. "Hey!" he said. "These two guys are still alive. Let's name them. How about G*rant*? That's an ant name."

Audrey folded her arms. "So is Sam*ant*ha."

"Those ants don't need names," Marvin said. "They need something *to do*." Then he unsnapped the green hatch door and squeezed in an eyedropper of sugar water. "I bet they're thirsty."

"You shouldn't open the ant farm without the teacher's permission," Audrey warned.

Just as Marvin tried to snap the lid back on, it dropped inside.

"OH NO, MARVIN!" shouted Audrey. "Now look what you've done! MRS. BIRD!"

Their teacher left the guinea pig committee and rushed over. "What's wrong?"

"MARVIN DROPPED THE LID IN THE ANT FARM!" Audrey yelled.

After a quick look, Mrs. Bird took the pencil off her ear and used it to try to scoop up the door. "I can't," she mumbled.

"Look out!" Fred said. "Grant and Samantha might get out."

"Who?"

"We named our ants," Fred explained.

Mrs. Bird smiled. Then she turned and scowled at Marvin. "Next time, wait for me before you open the cage."

By now, the goldfish, hamster, tadpole, and guinea pig committees had all left their tables and were watching Mrs. Bird. Mary Marony took one look at what their teacher was trying to do, and went back to the science cabinet.

The class watched Mrs. Bird uncoil a large paper clip. "If I can just snag that plastic hatch door . . ."

"Yes! You hooked it!" Audrey said.

"GRANT AND SAMANTHA ARE CRAWLING UP THE WALLS!" Fred yelled.

"I'm getting . . . it . . ." Mrs. Bird said.

"GO! GO! GO!" the class chanted.

Suddenly the green hatch door slipped off the paper-clip hook into the sand. "Oh, no . . ." Mrs. Bird groaned.

"Oh, no," the class echoed.

Mrs. Bird quickly reached for the book on the table, *Do Ants Wear Pants?*, and plopped it over the hatch hole.

"Phew!" she gasped as she sank into a nearby chair. "What are we going to do without that lid?"

"Use this one?" Mary Marony asked.

Everyone looked up.

Mary had a green hatch cover in her hand. "I took it off the old ant farm in the cabinet."

Mrs. Bird sighed. "I forgot all about that other ant farm. We used it last spring. Good for you, Mary!"

Elizabeth hugged Mary. "You saved the day!"

"Yippee for Mary!" Audrey cheered.

Marvin pointed to the ant farm. "Hey, look! Grant and Sam are playing seesaw on the green hatch door that fell in the sand."

When everyone laughed, Mrs. Bird shot Marvin a look. "Caring for classroom pets is a responsibility, Marvin

Higgins. Maybe you should think about it for a while at your desk. Alone."

Marvin trudged back to his seat. As he watched his ant committee having fun without him, he got a long face.

His teacher didn't like him.

She always picked on him.

Once again, Marvin remembered what his teacher had said about him after school.

Those *mean words*.

Marvin buried his head on his desk.

He felt like a dead ant.

2

Floss and Feathers

Marvin took out his pencil and note-book. He wrote the same sentence on each line.

I hate the teacher
I hate the teacher
I hate the teacher

"I'm glad to see you writing," Mrs. Bird said as she looked over at Marvin from across the room.

Marvin grinned. He felt a little bit better.

That afternoon the class made Happy Thanksgiving cards for their parents.

"Muh-mine isn't very good," Mary said.

"Yes it is, Muh-muh-mary," Marvin teased. He liked it when Mary Marony stuttered on M words. At least she wasn't perfect. Marvin knew Mrs. Bird thought she was.

Marvin looked at Mary's card. She had traced her hand on the cover and made a turkey. That was old, he

thought. Everyone did that in first grade.

Marvin held up his card. This was his chance to shine! He had the best card in the class. If only the teacher would notice, he thought.

"Your pumpkin pie is neat," Fred said.

"Like the whipped cream?" Marvin replied. "I just glued it on."

"Where did you get the cotton?" Pablo leaned over and asked.

Marvin lowered his voice. "It's not cotton. It's fish floss."

"Fish floss?" Fred asked.

"You know, that stuff Mrs. Bird puts in the fish filter."

"Ohhhh, wow!" Fred said.

"It's the extras that make a card," Marvin said.

Then he looked at Fred's turkey. "You should add a real feather."

Mary looked up. "There are feathers?"

Marvin got up. "Hang on," he said.

Mary and Fred watched Marvin walk over to the reading corner. Next to the big bookshelf was a hook. On the hook was an old feather duster.

FEATHERS!

Marvin pulled off two. He gave one fluffy orange feather to Mary and one to Fred.

"Thanks!" they said.

A few minutes later, the teacher stopped by Marvin's desk and touched the whipped cream on his card.

"Isn't that the fish floss that I put in our filter?"

Marvin nodded very slowly.

"Marvin! That is not for art projects."

"Sorry," Marvin mumbled. "Want me to put it back?"

"I don't think so," Mrs. Bird said. "There's glue all over it."

Marvin shrugged.

"Make sure you ask me before you take fish supplies. Okay?"

"Okay," Marvin replied. He was glad his pumpkin pie could keep its whipped cream.

The teacher didn't leave Marvin's desk, though. She kept staring at the card.

"Why did you write that to your parents?" she asked.

Marvin looked at his words:

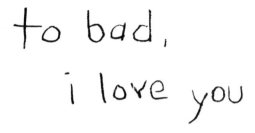

"What's wrong with it?"

Marvin noticed Mary and Fred were looking over his shoulder. "I made one card for my mom and one for my dad. This one is to my dad."

"Oh!" Mrs. Bird smiled and laughed gently. "You mean, 'To *Dad,* I love you.' "

"That's what I wrote!" Marvin replied.

Mrs. Bird lowered her voice. "You made a *b* instead of a *d*."

Marvin quickly reread his words, then reached for his pink eraser. His face felt like it was the same color of pink. He was so embarrassed!

Mrs. Bird patted him on the shoulder. "Amazing how a little thing like that can cause a misunderstanding. Everyone makes mistakes, Marvin. Don't feel bad."

Marvin continued to erase the *b* after the teacher left. He erased it so much he made a hole in his paper.

Marvin crumpled the card and threw it in the wastepaper basket. The teacher had made him goof up! Now he hated her more than anything.

Marvin opened his notebook and added something to his sentences.

I hate the teacher A HOLE LOT.
I hate the teacher A HOLE LOT.
I hate the teacher A HOLE LOT.

When he was on his tenth sentence, Mrs. Bird walked to the front of the room and asked the class to hold up their Thanksgiving cards. Everyone did, except Marvin. He had to sharpen his pencil.

"My goodness!" Mrs. Bird exclaimed. "Who brought in the beautiful feathers?"

Marvin looked at the turkey cards and grinned. Six had orange feathers.

Mary got up and walked the teacher back to the reading corner. "They came from . . . your feather duster."

Mrs. Bird looked at the plastic handle. There were only three feathers attached to it.

The class turned pin quiet.

Mrs. Bird shook her head and then burst out laughing. "So, *that's* what happened to my old feather duster."

As the class laughed with the teacher, Marvin continued to grind away at his pencil and wonder: *How come they could use stuff from the classroom and I couldn't?*

"We're sorry, Muh-mrs. Bird," Mary replied. "I'll bring another duster from home. It wasn't right. We need to replace it."

"Well," Mrs. Bird said, "I never knew an old feather duster could inspire so much writing. Your cards look great!"

When Mary returned to her seat, she looked at Marvin.

"You helped us muh-make great Thanksgiving cards. You make things fun, Muh-marvin."

"Thanks, Muh-muh-mary Muh-muh-marony."

Mary looked away. She was trying to be nice, and now Marvin was making fun of her stuttering.

Marvin folded his arms and sank down in his chair. For some reason it felt good to be mean to Mary.

3

Marvin Loses His Head

The next morning when Marvin walked into class, there was a glazed doughnut on a napkin and a paper cup filled with orange juice on everyone's desk.

"What's going on?" Marvin asked.

"A celebration!" Mrs. Bird said.

Mary jumped up and down.

"What for?" everyone said.

"The Whalers have finally won a game!" Mrs. Bird explained.

"Who are the Whalers?" Audrey asked.

"*Who are the Whalers?*" Pablo snapped. "What planet do *you* live on? They just happen to be the greatest hockey team in America."

Elizabeth rolled her eyes. "My mom and I are Bruins fans. They win a lot more games!"

Mrs. Bird put the score on the board:

Whalers 4
Bruins 2

While Pablo cheered and clapped, Elizabeth folded her arms.

When the bell rang, everyone raised his cup of juice. Mrs. Bird recognized

the fact that she had different fans in her room, so she made her toast: *"To hockey!"*

"To *THE WHALERS!*" Pablo yelled.

"*BRUINS!*" Elizabeth and Audrey replied.

Everyone drank his juice except Marvin.

"What's the matter, Marvin?" Mrs. Bird asked.

Marvin pushed his cup away. "I don't like orange juice."

"Well, you can enjoy your doughnut," Mrs. Bird said.

"I already had breakfast," Marvin grumbled.

Mrs. Bird sipped some juice. "You know, there's a player on the Whalers who has your name."

"Who?" Marvin asked.

"Joe Marvin."

"I don't know him," Marvin said. "Is he good?"

"GOOD? HE'S THE GREATEST!" Pablo yelled.

"He has a *temper*," Mrs. Bird added.

While the class was finishing the special snack, Mrs. Bird brought out a large print of a Norman Rockwell illustration.

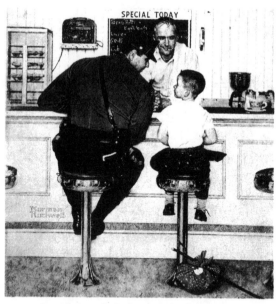

"Boys and girls, this is called *The Runaway*. We're going to see the original tomorrow when we take our field trip to Stockbridge, Massachusetts."

After the class cheered, Mrs. Bird asked, "Why do you think he's running away?"

"I bet his baby sister bugs him," Fred said.

Audrey raised her hand. "Maybe he didn't get one hundred on his spelling test."

"I know why," Pablo said. "He was playing hockey and he accidentally smashed the puck through the living room window. He didn't want to get punished, so he took off."

Marvin stared at the boy sitting at the lunch counter. At least *he* remembered to take his jacket.

While the class talked about art, Marvin's mind drifted back to . . .

. . . when he first heard those awful words.

Three days ago.

He remembered walking down the school hall. He didn't like being in the building after school, when no other kids were around.

Everything seemed so dark and quiet.

Even his footsteps echoed.

Why did he have to forget his jacket?

Marvin walked faster.

There it was!

Hanging up on the rack outside his classroom.

Marvin yanked it off the hanger.

As he was putting it on, he heard the teacher talking to the janitor.

*Saying those **mean words** . . .*

"I hate Marvin. He's a real trou-blemaker. I wish he'd just leave!"

Marvin took a quick peek. It was his teacher, Mrs. Bird . . . *talking about him!*

Marvin jumped back into the hall. He didn't want his teacher to know he had heard those mean words.

"Marvin? MARVIN?"

Marvin sat up in his chair. He had been deep in thought. Now his teacher was calling on him about the Norman Rockwell picture.

"Huh?"

"Why do *you* think the boy wants to run away?"

Marvin paused before he spoke. "Maybe . . . he thinks someone . . . *hates him*."

Mrs. Bird raised her eyebrows. "I wonder who that could be."

Marvin noticed that Audrey whispered something to Elizabeth. Then Elizabeth turned around and whispered something to Mary.

They were talking about him, he

thought. Marvin pulled his shirt up over his head. He felt like that boy in the painting. He wanted to run away too. His teacher wouldn't care. She *wanted* him to leave!

"Hey," Fred said. "You lost your head! Cool!"

Marvin let his shirt drop down to his eyeballs so he could check the time. He didn't feel cool at all. Just miserable.

He couldn't wait to go home.

4

Go Seek, and Hide

That afternoon when Marvin got home, he noticed a small trail of sand on the kitchen floor.

His grandmother must have changed the kitty litter, he thought.

"NONNA!" he called.

When there was no answer, Marvin walked into the living room. His grandmother was on the floor, peeking under the couch.

"What are you looking for, Nonna?"

When she still didn't answer, Marvin picked up the long cardboard tube that used to hold Christmas wrap and spoke into it. His grandmother was hard of hearing, and by using the tube, he didn't have to shout so much.

But, she did.

"What are you looking for, Nonna?"

"MY READING GLASSES."

Marvin kept frowning. "Yeah? So where's Ben, and when is Dad coming home?"

"YOUR BROTHER HAS PLAY PRACTICE AT THE HIGH SCHOOL. YOUR DAD'S GOING TO BE LATE. HE CALLED AND SAID FOR YOU AND ME TO GO AHEAD AND EAT DINNER. WANT TO PLAY AN EXCITING GAME OF HIDE AND GO SEEK?"

Marvin slowly started to smile. He hated it when his parents had gotten a divorce, two years ago, but he was used to it now. He saw his mother on the weekends, and during the week, he lived with his dad, his older brother, and now his grandmother. She had moved in last month. The best part of his day was playing games with Nonna. She could make a game out of anything.

Even lost glasses.

"Okay!" Marvin spoke into the tube. Then he paused. "How come you don't get a hearing aid, Nonna?"

"BECAUSE I DON'T WANT THAT THING IN MY EAR."

Marvin shook his head as his grandmother crawled over to the bookcase.

It was time to join her in a game of Hide and Go Seek. He got down on the floor and started looking for the gold-rimmed glasses.

He checked behind the TV.

He looked under a pile of newspapers.

He looked under the cushions on the couch.

No glasses!

Marvin plopped down on the couch
and spoke into the tube again. "Have
you ever had anyone say mean things
about you?"

Nonna crawled out from behind the
curtains and sat next to Marvin.

"YES. AND SOME OF THEM
HAVE BEEN RIGHT."

"Really?"

"SURE. I'M NOT PERFECT."

When Zeeber jumped on Nonna's lap, Nonna scratched his back with her long ruby-red nails.

"WHEN I WAS YOUR AGE, MARVIN, I LIVED ON A FARM. ONE DAY, I PUT A SNAKE IN MY FATHER'S MAILBOX. YOU SHOULD HAVE SEEN HIM JUMP WHEN HE PULLED HIS HAND OUT. HE HAD A FEW MEAN THINGS TO SAY ABOUT ME THAT NIGHT."

Marvin laughed. "And he was right."

"THAT TIME, YES."

Marvin watched Zeeber hop off Nonna's lap and walk into the kitchen. He could see the trail of kitty litter.

"THAT'S IT!"

"WHAT'S IT?"

"Follow me, Nonna!"

Marvin led his grandmother into the

laundry room. "There's one important place we haven't looked. There, under the sink!"

Nonna looked at the blue box. "I JUST CHANGED THE CAT LITTER. WHAT ABOUT IT?"

"I bet there's gold in that sand!"

Nonna bent down and looked. "MY GLASSES!"

After they laughed a good minute, the phone rang.

"I'll get it," Marvin said. "Hello? Hi, Dad. Yeah . . . uh-hun. Yeah . . . Oh, really? I . . . I understand. Okay. Bye."

Marvin sat down at the table and cupped his chin in his hand.

"WHAT'S THE MATTER?" Nonna asked.

Marvin put the tube next to his lips. "Dad was supposed to chaperone on my field trip to The Norman Rockwell Museum tomorrow, but . . . now he can't. Some dumb business has come up."

"I'LL GO WITH YOU."

Marvin stared at his grandmother. He wasn't sure he wanted her to come along. "It's just a bunch of art, Nonna. That's okay."

"BUT I LOVE NORMAN ROCK-WELL."

"You do?"

After Nonna rinsed her glasses, she joined Marvin at the kitchen table. "I SURE DO! I USED TO BUY THE *SATURDAY EVENING POST* MAGAZINE JUST BECAUSE IT HAD A NORMAN ROCKWELL COVER."

"You did?"

" 'COURSE IT ONLY COST FIFTEEN CENTS THEN. I CAN'T AFFORD TO BUY A MAGAZINE NOW...."

Marvin watched his grandmother move her chair, stand on it, and reach into a high cupboard. "SEE? HERE'S A PILE OF *SATURDAY EVENING POSTS*. I SAVED EVERY ONE THAT HAD A NORMAN ROCKWELL COVER. WANT TO SEE THEM?"

"Sure!" Marvin was amazed how his

40

grandmother knew where everything was in their house.

Except for her reading glasses.

He sure loved his grandmother. How could he tell her not to come on the field trip?

Marvin looked at the tube in his hand. What if she brought it along? Marvin knew he would *die* if he had to use it in front of his friends.

What could he do?

Suddenly an awful thought popped into Marvin's head.

He could hide that Christmas-wrap tube where *no one* would ever find it! He could do it when Nonna wasn't watching. Things get misplaced. Like glasses. Nonna's did!

"LOOK AT THIS COVER!" Nonna said. "MAY 23, 1953. *GIRL WITH A BLACK EYE.* THAT WAS ME AFTER

I PICKED A FIGHT WITH MY BROTHER. I'M TELLING YOU, I WAS NO ANGEL."

Marvin felt a little guilty when he laughed. He wasn't looking at the magazine. He was looking at the Christmas-wrap tube. Marvin knew *he* was no angel either.

5

Bus Disaster!

The next morning, Marvin and his grandmother walked down the school hall to his classroom. He carried their lunches in his book bag. The cold pack made it seem heavy.

Nonna wore a hat with three daisies on it. She said she didn't want any sun in her eyes. She also carried something under her arm.

Which was why Marvin was frowning.

"I'M SURE GLAD I HAD AN EXTRA CHRISTMAS-WRAP TUBE," Nonna said.

Marvin rolled his eyes. He had hidden the first one for nothing.

"Hey, Marv!" Fred said as he joined them. "Great day! The sun's shining, and I'm in your group. Where's your dad?"

"He couldn't come," Marvin grumbled. He didn't feel like introducing his grandmother to anybody. Not even to Fred.

"You must be Marvin's grandmother," Fred said.

"You have to raise your voice," Marvin groaned. "My grandmother is hard of hearing."

"Cool. HI, MRS. HIGGINS. I'M FRED. WHAT'S THAT TUBE FOR?"

"IF ANYONE FOOLS AROUND, I'LL BOP THEM ONE."

Then she bonked Marvin's head with it.

Plonk!

Fred cracked up.

Marvin stared straight ahead.

When they got to the classroom, they saw the other chaperones. They all looked like young mothers to Marvin. No one had white hair or rounded shoulders like his grandmother.

And *no one* had such a LOUD VOICE!

Why did she have to come, anyway? Marvin thought.

"Mrs. Higgins! How nice you could come in Mr. Higgins's place," Mrs. Bird said.

Fred spoke up right away. "You have to raise your voice when you talk to Marvin's grandmother. She's hard of hearing."

"Oh," Mrs. Bird said. "I'M GLAD YOU COULD COME, MRS. HIG-GINS."

"GLAD TO BE HERE. SHOULD WE GO TO THE BATHROOM NOW, OR DO THEY HAVE BATH-ROOMS AT THE MUSEUM?"

Marvin stepped behind his grand-mother. He didn't want anyone to see his red face.

"THERE ARE NICE CLEAN BATH-ROOMS AT THE MUSEUM," Mrs. Bird shouted.

Fred Heinz slapped his knee. "Your granny is something!"

"Her name is *Nonna*," Marvin snapped.

As the children began boarding the bus, Mrs. Bird reminded them, "Two on a seat, please."

Audrey, Elizabeth, and Mary frowned.

Marvin and Fred raced to the back of the bus. Nonna sat across the aisle from them in a seat by herself.

After fifteen minutes on the road, the boys made their first big sighting.

"Look, there's a farm. We're getting close to the Massachusetts border."

Suddenly all the children groaned and held their noses. "Eeeeeweyee!"

49

"WHY ALL THE SCREAMING?"
Nonna asked.

"CAN'T YOU SMELL THE COW
MANURE?" Marvin replied.

"JUST A MINUTE, THE BUS IS
TOO NOISY. I CAN'T HEAR YOU."

Marvin watched his grandmother
pull out the wrapping-paper tube and
hold it next to her ear. "Huh?"

Marvin froze.

He couldn't do it.

Not in front of his friends.

They'd make fun of him.

When Marvin pushed the tube away, Nonna got the message. She laid the tube down next to her on the seat. Then she took out a book and her glasses and began reading.

Marvin looked at Mary and Elizabeth in front of him. They didn't notice anything. They were too busy singing with Audrey and Emmy Sue across the aisle.

"Was that supposed to be a hearing-aid phone?" Fred giggled.

Marvin turned. "You saw?"

"How could I miss? What a crack up!"

Crack up? Marvin thought. *What a disaster.*

Then Fred made a horn out of both his hands and shouted in Marvin's ear,

"HEY, SONNY, THIS IS YOUR GRANNY. I CAN'T HEAR YOU."

The girls stopped singing and turned around.

"Stop that!" Marvin growled. "Don't you know it's mean to make fun of people who are hard of hearing?"

Fred raised his eyebrows. "Really? How come it's okay for you to make fun of people who stutter?"

When Marvin saw Mary looking at him, he scooted down in his bus seat.

Maybe Mrs. Bird was right to hate him. He did make fun of Mary. He knew he didn't like Fred when he made fun of Nonna.

The next moment, while Marvin was deep in thought, something happened.

The bus stopped in the middle of the road.

Pablo stood up, unlocked a window,

and poked his head out. "Cars and trucks are lined up for about a mile."

"I bet a car hit a cow," Fred said, jumping up.

"PLEASE SIT DOWN," Mrs. Bird called from the front of the bus. "THE BUS DRIVER IS RADIOING AHEAD. WE SHOULD FIND OUT WHAT THE PROBLEM IS SHORTLY. IN THE MEANTIME, PLEASE STAY IN YOUR SEATS."

Marvin looked out the window. This field trip was supposed to be fun. Not one disaster after another.

6

Tube Talk

Pablo took out his pocket radio. "Maybe I can find out something on the news about the accident."

"Look!" Emmy Sue said. "A helicopter from the television station is on its way. See the cameras?"

"Listen to all those sirens!" Fred said.

Marvin turned around and looked out the back window of the bus. "It's a fire engine and two police cars coming up the shoulder of the road."

Nonna leaned over the aisle. "WHAT'S GOING ON?"

"NO ONE KNOWS YET, NONNA," Marvin shouted.

Then Mrs. Bird stood up. "THE BUS DRIVER JUST GOT NEWS THAT THERE HAS BEEN AN ACCIDENT."

Everyone in the bus gasped.

"APPARENTLY, THEY HAVE TO CLEAR THE ROAD BEFORE WE CAN MOVE ON. IT WILL BE ABOUT A FIFTEEN-MINUTE WAIT."

"I wish I was in that helicopter filming the cleanup. That would be the greatest!" Pablo said.

"That would be awful," Audrey replied.

Mary Marony covered her eyes. "What if someone got killed?"

Fred pressed his nose to the window. "We can't see the fire engine or police cars anymore. What are we going to do for fifteen minutes? Look at the cows in the pasture?"

Marvin looked over at his grandmother. She had set her book on her lap. The Christmas tube was still on the seat next to her.

"TIME FOR A GAME, MARVIN?" she asked.

Yes!

Marvin stood up. He didn't care what Mrs. Bird thought anymore. "I know what we can do while we're waiting," he said to his classmates. "How many of you know how to play Telephone?"

"That's boring," Fred groaned.

Marvin reached over and grabbed the tube. "This is a different kind of Telephone," he said. "It's called . . . Tube

Talk. My grandmother and I play it a lot."

Everyone watched Marvin hold up the long cardboard cylinder and talk into it. "Okay," he continued. "I'll start a message and we'll see how it comes out. If you don't get it right, I'll bop you on the head."

When everyone laughed, Marvin

smiled. He liked thinking of fun things to do.

Mrs. Bird wasn't smiling, though. Marvin guessed she didn't like the bopping part of the game.

Marvin whispered something in Fred's ear. Fred took the cardboard roll and whispered through it into Pablo's ear. Pablo held it next to Mary's ear,

and Mary continued. By the time the Tube Talk went all around the bus, Emmy Sue stood up and repeated the message.

"This is what I got," Emmy Sue said. *"I hope Nonna doesn't get a dent in her hat."*

Marvin laughed. "NO! It was supposed to be . . . I HOPE *NO ONE* GOT HURT IN THE *ACCIDENT.*"

Lots of kids clapped when Marvin bopped Emmy Sue on the head three times.

As they played a few more rounds of Tube Talk in the bus, Marvin thought about words.

He loved funny ones. Why did there have to be mean ones? Marvin remembered how he cried that day when he heard Mrs. Bird talking to the janitor.

Once again, he recalled each mean word she had said about him: *"I hate Marvin. I wish he'd leave. He always spoils everything."*

When Marvin looked around the bus, everyone was having fun. They liked his game. He wondered if Mrs. Bird still felt the same way she did three days ago. Maybe there was time to change her mind.

Now it was Marvin's turn to tell the phone message. He stood up and tried to repeat what Fred had started. *"I smell cow doo-doo in the pasta?"*

Mrs. Bird shook her head.

After everyone laughed, Fred jumped up and bopped Marvin on the head. "NO! NO! It's supposed to be . . . I SMELL COWS IN THE *PASTURE*. *DO* **YOU**?"

"Ohhhh!" the kids replied.

"LOOK!" Mary shouted. "THE TRAFFIC IS STARTING TO MUH-MUH-MOVE AGAIN."

Marvin didn't make fun of Mary's stuttering this time. He just looked out the window at the long row of cars, trucks, and motorcycles that had started their engines.

After the bus moved along the road for about a mile, everyone could see what had caused the traffic jam.

A truck carrying Pampers had over-turned, and there were hundreds of paper diapers pushed to the side of the road.

"WAS ANYONE HURT?" Nonna asked. Marvin put the Christmas-wrap tube next to her ear. Using it wasn't a big deal anymore.

"No one was hurt, Nonna," he said.

"Ahhhhh, good!" Mary sighed.

Fred looked out his window. "Hey! Can we pull over? My mom could use some of those diapers for my baby sister."

Everyone looked at the pink and blue boxes as the bus passed by.

Except for Audrey. She had a message from Mrs. Bird for Marvin. "The teacher wants to have *a word with you* before you go into the museum."

A word with me? Marvin thought.

He knew what that meant.

Trouble!

When the bus arrived at the museum, Marvin stayed at the end of the line. He followed his classmates slowly up the white stone path. The Norman Rockwell Museum looked like a ghostly mansion to Marvin.

He could see Mrs. Bird waiting for him on the veranda. She was talking with Pablo.

Suddenly Pablo shouted, "MARVIN IS SUSPENDED!"

7

Teacher Showdown

Suspended?

Marvin started to tremble. So that's why Mrs. Bird wanted to see him before the tour. She was going to kick him out of second grade!

Marvin watched Nonna lead Emmy Sue and Mary to the girls' bathroom just inside the lobby. Mrs. Bird was still standing on the veranda, waiting for him.

Marvin didn't want to see his teacher. He had to think fast.

"Marvin!" Mrs. Bird called. "I need to talk to you."

Marvin dashed into the building. "I have to go, Mrs. Bird. Excuse me!"

Mrs. Bird shrugged, mentioned something to a chaperone, and then went to the lobby desk to handle details about the class tour.

When Marvin came out of the boys' bathroom, he joined the class. *Saved,* he thought. *At least for an hour.* Mrs. Bird couldn't talk to him very well on the tour.

Marvin sat down with the rest of the class on the mossy green rug in front of a large painting. He made a point *not* to sit near Pablo, who was whispering something to Audrey.

Marvin stared straight ahead at the

gray-haired tour guide. She was just about the same age as Nonna, he thought.

Nonna and Mrs. Bird were sitting on a bench behind the class. Everyone was quiet.

"This is one of Norman Rockwell's most famous illustrations," the guide said. "It's called *Surprise.*

"Can anyone guess what the story might be in this picture?"

While Marvin studied the painting, Fred raised his hand. "It's the teacher's birthday. The kids wrote 'Happy Birthday' on the board. Some of them gave her gifts. You can see them on her desk."

Elizabeth pointed to the boy with the eraser on his head. "I think it was his idea to surprise the teacher."

Instead of blurting something out the way he usually did, Marvin raised his hand politely. "I agree with Elizabeth. It was Eraser Head who thought of writing 'Happy Birthday' and 'Surprise' all over the board."

When Marvin said "Eraser Head," the guide chuckled.

"But . . . he didn't write those words for his teacher. He just wanted to cover up all those math problems. Now they don't have to do them."

The guide nodded. "Hmmmm, so Eraser Head has a devilish streak?"

"Yeah," Marvin groaned. "Kind of like me. But mine's getting smaller," he added.

When Marvin turned around, he noticed Mrs. Bird was smiling.

Was there still a chance? he wondered.

Then he noticed something else.

An empty space beside Mrs. Bird.

Where was Nonna?

After the class had finished talking about another Norman Rockwell illustration, and Marvin listened politely, Nonna was still missing.

"Where could she be?" Marvin asked Fred.

Fred shrugged. "Probably in the john."

Marvin looked at his watch. "For six and a half minutes?"

"Sometimes it takes a while to take care of business."

Marvin scowled. Right when he was scoring points with his teacher, he had a tough decision to make. Look for Nonna, or stay put and be polite.

Marvin made his choice.

He ducked out the front museum room and into the lobby. After he took a quick look in the souvenir shop, he checked out the stairwell leading to the basement. *Oh no,* he thought. *She couldn't be . . .*

Marvin dashed down the steps.

Phew! he thought. No dead body at the bottom of the stairs.

Marvin went back upstairs, and stood near the ladies' room. "Excuse me," he said to a woman entering the lounge. "Could you tell me if my grandmother is in there? She's wearing a daisy hat."

"I'll check," the woman said.

Moments later, the woman stuck her head out the door. "She's not in here."

Marvin's heart beat faster.

He had to find her.

But where?

He looked out the glass door. Who was that walking toward the museum?

A lady with a daisy hat!

It had to be Nonna, he thought.

When he felt a tap on the shoulder, he jumped. "MRS. BIRD!"

"I don't remember your asking me for permission to go to the bathroom," she said sternly.

Marvin looked at the men's room sign above him. "Eh . . . I'm sorry. Real sorry. I should have asked. But Nonna was . . ."

Marvin looked out the glass door again. It *was* his grandmother. "Right here!"

"Nonna?" Mrs. Bird said, turning her

head. "Oh, yes. Well, if you were with an adult, that's okay."

Marvin wiped his brow. *That was a close one!* he thought. Now, if he could just rejoin the group with Nonna. Marvin started to move away.

"Did you get my message that I wanted to talk to you?" Mrs. Bird asked.

Marvin froze. *The moment alone with her had arrived!*

Time for a *showdown* with his teacher.

"Yes?" Marvin squeaked. His tennis shoes started to tap the shiny slate floor. He couldn't stay calm. He was about to be suspended. It was like getting his head chopped off, or being executed in a firing squad. His life was over.

As a second-grader.

Mrs. Bird looked him square in the eye. "Marvin, you know that game you organized in the bus?"

"Ye-yes," Marvin stuttered.

"I loved it! You took a difficult situation and made it fun. I appreciate how you kept the class calm."

"Calm?" Marvin's shoes started doing a tap dance. "Wasn't there something else you wanted to tell me?"

Mrs. Bird shook her head.

Marvin had to be sure. "What about what you said Monday after school *about me*."

Mrs. Bird wrinkled her eyebrows. "About you? Monday after school?"

"You said . . ." Marvin couldn't help the way his voice cracked. He had to say those *mean words*. When his eyes filled up with water, he quickly wiped them

with his shirtsleeve. ". . . you . . . hated
me and wished I would . . . leave."

There! He said it.

Mrs. Bird's voice squeaked, "Oh,
Marvin, I would never say that about
you."

"But you did! I heard you."

Mrs. Bird tugged at her red hair. "I

said the name Marvin? Oh . . . *Marvin!* I was talking about *Joe Marvin,* the hockey player. His temper tantrums were spoiling the team. I said I hoped *he* would leave! Not *you.* You're my class leader!"

Marvin's eyes bulged. "You were talking about *some hockey player?*"

Mrs. Bird nodded. "Pablo just heard on his radio that he was suspended from the Whalers today!"

So that was it! Marvin wanted to scream YAHOO! but he was in a museum. Instead he jumped in the air and slapped the men's room sign a high five.

"I feel like doing a high five too," Mrs. Bird said. "Now maybe the Whalers can win some more games."

"All right!" Marvin said, slapping his teacher's hand.

Just then Nonna opened the glass
door and greeted both of them. When
Mrs. Bird returned to the class, Marvin
made a deep sigh.

He was safe as a second-grader after
all!

"SO," he said, "*WHERE DID YOU
GO? I'VE BEEN LOOKING ALL
OVER FOR YOU.*"

Nonna opened her purse. "AND WHO ARE YOU? MY BODY-GUARD?"

"YUP!"

Nonna took out her gold-rimmed glasses. "I CAN'T READ THE BLURBS UNDER THE PAINTINGS WITHOUT THESE. I LEFT THEM ON THE BUS SEAT."

Marvin rolled his eyes. "I SHOULD HAVE GUESSED! WELL, THANKS FOR SHOWING UP WHEN YOU DID. MRS. BIRD THINKS I LEFT THE GROUP WITH YOU."

"SHE DOES, HUH?"

"YUP."

Nonna poked Marvin in the chest with her glasses. "ARE YOU GOING TO DO SOMETHING DUMB LIKE THAT AGAIN?"

"NO WAY."

Then Marvin paused. "ARE YOU GOING TO TELL?"

"NO . . . I GUESS NOT." Nonna gave Marvin a long hug. "I TOLD YOU I'M NO ANGEL."

Marvin grinned as he hugged his grandmother back. "ME EITHER."